YASHEWE

(YA-SHE-WAY)

S.D. MCGUIRE

Copyright © 2020, Grumpy Ogre Press

All rights reserved. No part of this publication may be reproduced, distributed, or transmitted in any form or by any means, including photocopying, recording, or other electronic or mechanical methods, without the prior written permission of the publisher, except in the case of brief quotations embodied in critical reviews and certain other noncommercial uses permitted by copyright law.

This is a work of fiction. Any characters, names, places, or likenesses are purely fictional. Resemblances to any of the items listed above are merely coincidental.

Second Edition
ISBN (PB): 978-1-952051-00-5

(First Edition) ISBN: 9781099129919
Imprint: Independently published

Designed by Sophia LeRoux

Yashewe Illustration (Ch. 8) by Erick "Dub" Weir

S.D. MCGUIRE BOOKS

The Final Cut

The Unnameable War

Grisly Maze (COMING SOON)

Sonar Prey (COMING SOON)

Acknowledgements

This book is dedicated to the people of the Indian Nations whom I hold very dear to my heart. They are my mother's people and I hope the grandfathers and grandmothers long since gone, walk with me through my journey of enlightenment.

Author's note

So it appears we dance again, my wonderful friends, as you are about to step onto the stage of book two in my horror short series titled *The Tombstone Shorts*.

It appears that you have lived through "The Final Cut" and are willing to continue your journey into the horrific mind of S.D. McGuire.

With each book you read, my hope is that you will lose a little more of your sanity, to where at the end you will join me six feet down as we read together!

S.D. McGuire

CHAPTER ONE

"What do you mean we can't go any further through the gorge? My rails are gonna go from here to Frisco, young man, so don't tell me we have to stop here on account of some dead Injuns! Do you know who I am? I'm Robert Moore. You see the letters on the side of the caboose, son? '*R & M Rail*'. That stands for Robert and Munroe Railroad, and that's me, boy! Don't be tellin' me what I ain't gonna do, you got it?" Moore smoothed down the front of his dark green silk jacket, brushing off a stray piece of soot that had blown into the coach car from somewhere, looked at his gold pocket watch that sat on the table for a moment, then picked it up and rubbed the Celtic cross embellishment fondly before putting it in his breast pocket.

Looking at Timmy disdainfully, he bit down angrily on the stump of his Irish cigar. "Now you go tell that conductor Delbert Jenkins that this here train is gonna go through that God-cursed gorge. We gotta get to that depot afore next Tuesday to deliver these rails; we can't extend this railway out until they get them. Now, I know my partner Jacob is a Scotsman and they tend to believe such wild tales, but I'll be hearing no more ignorant talk of spirits and ghosts, boy. Now GO!" With a wave of his hand, Moore went back to his chess game with the engineer, Ford Smith.

Ford, dressed in his customary black and gray engineer's suit, adjusted his crisp black cap further down on his head and pretended to concentrate on the game in front of him. Moore didn't pay the boy any more attention, even as the tall, blond-haired youth dressed in dirty gray coveralls stood for a moment shaking his head, then finally turned and headed up the aisle towards the door to the coal car.

***

Timmy Lufton was an engineer's helper here on the R&M Railroad, but he was certainly no fool for his 18 years. He had heard the stories from old hobos like Tibbets and Cotton Shackleford about something killing the White people heading west on the trains, and he didn't want to push his luck. He knew enough about Injuns to know they were pretty mad about being shoved further and further west.

R&M were running the rails straight through the heart of Cheyenne country, and Robert Moore and Jacob Munroe had been warned about the old Indian burial ground in the gorge. But Robert Moore—being the greedy Irishman he was—was hell bent on bringing not only the White man but the

Bible with him to get rid of these savages, and had ignored all the warnings from the local trappers and scouts that knew the area.

Nine months ago, they had deliberately laid track down through what was now called Dead Gorge. It had been a Cheyenne Indian burial place for centuries, or so it was told, and as they did, they had disturbed something that even the Indians were afraid of. They called it Yashewe, and it had horribly butchered at least twenty Whites since that first track was laid. The local Army post Commander had fobbed it off as just another Indian uprising, protesting the loss of their lands, but Timmy believed the stories old Cotton would tell late at night after he had been tempted with a bottle of sour mash.

Cotton had never seen the beast, but he had heard a tale of four White soldiers who had been walking the tracks nearby late at night, looking for a runaway scout. Word had it that all four men had been well-armed and on horseback. When they went missing, the Army post twenty miles away at Caleb's Creek had sent out a search party. What they found had been kept secret—or so they thought. Cotton had been at the post when the search party had returned. They had only two horses with them, and a bloody bag tied around one of them. Cotton said the men in that search party had immediately gone into the small saloon on post and started drinking. Naturally enough, Cotton was there to help aid in their downing several bottles of rot-gut whiskey, after which one of the men had related to Cotton what they had found.

Apparently, the search party had figured the men would head down the tracks looking for the missing Indian scout, since that would be the easiest way through the valley. After they had traveled almost to within sight of the gorge, they had decided to go on foot so they could see the tracks better.

After a few miles, they had spotted two horses standing beside the tracks. As the search party moved towards the horses, they figured the animals would bolt and head the other way, but the minute the horses spotted the searchers, they flew across the ground towards them. When they got to the men, the horses stopped and seemed to calm down. They were sweating and foaming at the mouth, as if they had been running all night without stopping, and had dried blood caked on their backs and down their legs.

At first, the men had thought the horses had been cut on the jagged rocks and briars all along the gorge rails, but after inspecting them, it became evident that they were not cut anywhere. Seeing this as a bad omen, some of the searchers wanted to turn back, but they voted to continue on until at least the edge of the gorge.

After only a few thousand feet past where they had found the horses, they saw some strange tracks in the gravel underneath the iron train track, leading away from the rails. A stone's throw from the tracks, they found what the soldier described to Cotton as 'the Devil's supper table'. Two horses and the four soldiers had been completely torn apart and almost completely eaten. They had salvaged the torso of one of the men—which was what they had brought back in the bloody burlap sack.

Cotton said the man told him that whatever had killed those men was huge and walked on two feet but left no tracks that they had ever seen before. There were teeth and claw marks in the bones of the dead victims that could not have been made by a mountain lion, or even a bear, and from the way the bodies had been torn apart and mangled, none of the searchers believed it was Indians. The dead men's skulls had been completely smashed in, and there was not enough flesh on the bones to have fed a dog.

Arms were torn and broken, hands missing fingers, yet the horses were not as badly mangled as the men, which the searchers found odd. It was though they had been scared to death, though they had a few claw marks on them as evidence something horrific had attacked them. Despite the searchers' claims, the Commander had ordered the locals be told it was Indians who had attacked, as this was less fantastical but still enough to keep the settlers afraid of going out on their own at night.

Timmy shuddered at the memory of how even old Cotton seemed spooked about riding the rails these days. Still, he had a job to do and he kept his thoughts to himself as he moved through the coach door onto the coal car siding.

CHAPTER TWO

The thunderclouds in the distance coupled with the steam from the sitting train, made the landscape even gloomier, Timmy thought. As he worked his way through huge piles of coal towards the front of the train, he wondered if the whole of the west was like this; barren and deserted except for the occasional tree or small mountain. Climbing over the last mound of black, dusty coal, Timmy saw the brown haired, ruddy looking but well-built Mr. Jenkins leaning up against the huge control panel, packing his pipe as usual. Delbert was wearing his normal conductor's overalls—black with gold trim—and the black top hat he preferred to wear. With all the cold wind that had been blowing about, the soot from the engine furnace had covered him in a light gray dusting.

Timmy had always been fascinated by the many knobs and gauges and handles on the steam engine's vast control plate. Mr. Jenkins was a mild-mannered but capable conductor and was often in the mood to show Timmy just how things ran. One day, Timmy hoped he would be able to run this train as well as the conductor.

Jenkins saw him climb over the coal and smiled, "Why there you are, son! I thought Mr. Moore had thrown you offen the train. What did old Money Pants have to say about not going any further? Let me see, something about this costing him money, stupid Injuns holding everything up, and you better git up here and tell me to get going. Does that sound about right?"

With a sly wink, Jenkins laughed as Timmy just nodded his head.

***

Delbert Jenkins had been a steam engine conductor on some of the best railroads in the east. The only reason he had taken this job was the bonus that R&M Railroad had offered to any persons willing to try and push the tracks all the way West. With all the Indian uprisings, not many had the grit to take this kind of a job on, but Delbert's mild manner hid a stubborn and tenacious side. Delbert's 20 years as a train conductor had taught him a great many things. Having served with the Union Army out of Fort Lookout and fought in several engagements during the recent war, Delbert—as well as Jacob Munroe—thought he was the ideal man to take on a job such as this. Robert Moore, however, was of the opinion that Delbert was far too sympathetic with the savage Indians, as he had taken a squaw wife at one point. Moore was a devout Catholic, and thought all Indian savages should have the weight of the Lord beaten into them.

"Timmy, I suspect you oughta shovel a few rounds of that black gold yonder in ol' Miss Emily here so's we can get up some steam, then you best be getting back to the caboose and get them hobos broke up and offen that bottle I know they have stashed back there. We don't want Mr. Moore finding out they have laid away on this train again, or he will throw them off in the middle of nowhere. You know how his temper is. And when you see him, tell that so-called engineer Ford Smith that he best be greasing them wheels again. That right rear one has been settin' up an awful squeaking. Been scaring them buffalo all over the territory," Delbert said with a snort.

Turning back to the controls, Delbert pulled his top hat down on his forehead, then put his right hand on the long brass handle going across the front of the control panel.

Easing the lever catch back, he slowly started pulling back on the handle as the steam rushed through the engine to take hold.

***

After a few seconds, the loud puff that Timmy loved was heard as the huge piston turned over, and the large rotators on either side of the engine started their relentless revolutions of the massive steel wheels. The engine lurched forward like some great sleeping behemoth being rudely awakened and the train started its jerky forward momentum as Timmy headed back to the rear of the line of cars. He decided to go up on top, even though Delbert had warned him not to. He didn't want to go back through the club car with Mr. Moore in it. The rich man had no use for anyone on this train, and especially not the hobos. They were beneath the likes of men like him, and Mr. Moore made sure everyone knowed it.

Timmy climbed up the heavy metal ladder to the top of the coach car and started walking shakily back down the train. He always loved being on top of the trains; it made him feel like he was flying. Delbert would chastise him for walking on the roof like this, but he knew the other man would be occupied with getting the train underway. Delbert had warned him that out in Indian territory, they took shots at any fool walking out in the open. One day, he always said, Timmy was gonna get an arrow right though his brisket if he didn't watch out.

As the train slowly moved through the dry, grassy plain, Timmy saw rain in the distance. He always wondered why it was so dry out here, because when it rained, it seemed to rain enough to flood the world and wash away all the Whites and Indians alike, but yet when done, there would be hardly any signs of it's coming.

The long metal centipede was moving now; its telltale rhythmic click on the tracks and the steady loud huff of steam from the smokestack filling the air. Timmy would often lie up here at night, look at the stars wondering what America had been like before the White man came, and then fall asleep to the comforting sound.

Now though, the biting cold forced him to move quickly, and it didn't take him long to cross the two coach cars and reach the first flatbed with stacks of iron track rails on it. The train held five of the long flatbed cars, and all stacked as high as could be reached with railroad ties and iron rails; enough to stretch more of the railroad's spidery frame across the Indian nations. Enough to cause even more unrest and resentment from the native peoples.

Timmy had been taught that the Indians were savages, and they had no right to own this land, but Timmy knew that the main reason the White men said such things was because they wanted to take the land from the Indians, which he also knew was wrong, but he was only one boy among thousands and could not change anything. He remembered getting beaten by the preacher at the Wheelock School for defending an Indian boy against the preacher's cruel whip.

The preacher had been beating a small, inoffensive Indian named Two Fox for not speaking the White name that had been given to him by the preacher. Timmy had been taller than most children, and his classmates had looked to him as a natural leader. He had only withstood watching a couple of lashes fall on the back of the stoic Two Fox before jumping up and grabbing the whip from the preacher's hand, and then throwing it out the window of the small wood frame schoolhouse. That boy later became blood brothers with Timmy, and they had even performed a sacred ritual, cutting their palms and joining their hands together so that their blood would mingle freely and they would become one. Timmy had been very proud of that moment. Two Fox was his Cheyenne blood brother now, but Timmy had not seen him for four years. He was either dead, or somewhere out here in the vast plains and low rolling mountains.

As Timmy navigated his way through the stacks of wooden railroad cross ties and iron rails, he automatically checked the ropes and chains to make sure none of the load had shifted or worked its way loose. Secretly, he wished he could just cut the whole load loose and let it tumble onto the plains, spoiling R&M's plans to stretch the White man across the whole nation; but he needed this job, so he held his desires in check.

Reaching the end of the flatbed cars, he jumped over onto the bright red caboose trimmed with gold and black. Timmy often wondered if the reason the buffalo would sometimes charge at the trains was because of the bright red cabooses at the rear of this loud, steaming animal travelling at high speed across their grasslands. Something about red seemed to enrage the giant creatures, and Timmy had seen them kill themselves intentionally by throwing their great bulks against the moving trains more than once. It was if the very land itself hated the coming of the White man…

CHAPTER THREE

Checking the connections to the caboose and making sure all was secure, as was his habit, Timmy opened the creaky wooden door to the caboose and walked in. Beside the old rusted and potbellied iron stove were two disheveled and definitely ripe old hobos—Cotton Shackleford and Tibbets—along with the coal man, Frank Rizzo.

Cotton in particular was the essence of the classic hobo; with a face so old and wrinkled his age could only be guessed at. He had a constantly smiling wide mouth with crooked teeth that were yellowed from years of tobacco chewing, a patchwork brown jacket and pants along with a raggedy red shirt with stains on it. To top it off, he wore a black cap that was so old and worn out it was amazing it would even stay on his head. And rounding out his hobo guise, he had a long, dirty white beard that always seemed to have some sort of food or tobacco stuck to it.

Tibbets was a peaceful Black man of around fifty or so, of average build with short gray hair, a dirty black suit that looked to be two sizes too big, and the enormous boots he always wore. The other thing about Tibbets was that he was mute, having had his tongue cut out by white soldiers long ago. One curious thing about Tibbets was that he never went anywhere without Cotton; the two men seemed to look out for each other.

The three men were all drinking from a worn-out old amber bottle of sour mash whiskey and playing cards on the little wooden crate in front of them.

"Well, well, lookie here, if it ain't Lil Iron Britches hisself!" Cotton said, grinning at the youth.

"Shucks Cotton, you know I ain't no iron britches, but y'all better straighten up and get scarce if Mr. Moore comes back this way, He'll throw all y'all offen this train lickety split!"

***

Frank Rizzo cast a warning glance over at Timmy, "Now boy, don't you go getting your knickers all in a twist over that fat cat in there. We got a job to do, and we is going to make sure we git it done. You leave the man stuff to us, ya hear?"

Cotton elbowed the coal man in the ribs and laughed, "Frank, now you best be getting up there and slinging that black gold in the fires of Hell to move this train faster through this here Injun territory, or you'll be et up just like the rest of us!"

Frank stood up and glared at Cotton, and then at Timmy with his dark, often menacing eyes.

Rizzo was of Italian descent and had a mean temper, liking no one on the train, it seemed. The only thing he did like was gambling and drinking. He had no use for hobos, but they were the only ones he could beat at poker. Rizzo stretched his six foot frame slowly, then hitched up his dirty gray coveralls covered in coal dust, moved his dark blue cap around on his unruly black haired head for a minute, and then eased past Timmy with a snort and headed out the door towards the front of the train. Frank Rizzo was the coal man, and his sole job was to ensure there was a steady stream of coal being fed into the greedy furnace of the train to keep the wheels rolling. It was a hard, thankless job, but Frank liked it—stoking the fires seemed to fuel his own inner fires somehow Timmy thought to himself.

***

Timmy turned towards Cotton and Tibbets, then moved over to where Frank had been sitting on the small wooden nail keg and sat down. As he warmed his hands by the stove, they all sat in silence for a few moments before Cotton spoke up.

"Well, boy, don't look like ol' Iron Hide is going to take any heed of the killings, is he? Looks to me like he is planning on trying to go through the gorge, and hit a coming storm at that. We get broke down in thar, and mark my words, we is all going to be pushing up daisies afore long. Them there Injun spirits is gonna come for us the way they done all the rest, and ain't nothing gonna stop em!"

As Cotton finished speaking, he looked over at Tibbets, who merely nodded in agreement as usual. Tibbets went wherever Cotton did, and Timmy had never seen them far apart. There was some sort of mutual understanding between the two itinerant men. They looked out for one another on the tracks, and each made sure the other was included in any food found or handouts taken. Cotton tolerated Tibbets' Bible-abiding ways, and Tibbets didn't seem to mind the old White hobo's predilection for stealing food and whisky from the local merchants—being quite good at it himself when the need arose.

Cotton reached for the bottle of rot-gut whiskey he had filched from the store back on the post and handed it over to Timmy, who took it with an almost air of pride in being offered the bottle. Wiping off the mouth of the dusty, dark glass bottle, he tried one small sip of the burning liquid before choking, then handed the bottle quickly over to Tibbets, who merely smiled and put the cork back in it, and then tucked the bottle away in his jacket.

Cotton slapped Timmy on the back and laughed heartily, "You know, boy, you just don't seem like you're gonna make a good hobo. You better stick to these trains to make a livin'!"

Timmy nodded, eyes watering, and then stood up slowly. "Cotton, I gots to be getting back up to the front, you'uns better keep your eye out. Don't get caught in here; I'd hate for y'all to get throwed offen this train out here in the middle of nowhere." Timmy set four biscuits and a piece of side meat on the crate and winked at the two old men. "And here, ol' Rich Britches won't miss a few biscuits now and then."

Cotton looked at the boy gravely for a moment, then nodded and reached out and took Timmy's hand in his. After holding it firmly for a moment, he let go and turned to the crate laden with food.

CHAPTER FOUR

Delbert eased the train through the plains at a steady trot; trying to keep the reserve steam for if they needed it. He didn't want to get caught out here at night, and he planned on clearing the gorge as quickly as possible. Whether they were stories or not, he didn't want no truck with a raiding party of Cheyenne—or worse, Sioux. He knew what they were capable of, and to them, this train was as bad a medicine as you could get. It was the reason so many of them had been killed and starved out; and perhaps, if the stories were all true, maybe this train was also the reason something was killing off all the White people that came near Dead Gorge. Whatever it was, it was not something Delbert wished to tackle without an army behind him. He rubbed the wooden handle of the Colt revolver stowed in its holster on his belt, looking out of the side of the car at the ever approaching storm clouds, and then at the rising mountains that were the backdrop to the gorge up ahead. Yes, whatever it was, he wanted no truck with it.

"Hey Delbert, you gonna open this old bitch up and get us through the gorge afore daybreak, or are you plannin' on gettin' yourself another squaw and settlin' down here?" Frank yelled from the coal pile, where he was using a wooden stave with a hook on one end to pull down coal from the top onto a smaller pile, this in an effort to make his job easier.

As Frank picked up a load of the black rock on his shovel and started for the coal door on the engine, Delbert whipped out his pistol in the blink of an eye and pointed it smoothly at Frank's head. "I've told you once before, Rizzo, don't be calling Miss Emily here any harsh names, or you will be sitting dead on the tracks as she rolls away from your body! It is bad luck to lay curses on the train you are working and living on, I done told you that. Don't make me tell you again!"

Delbert's eyes flashed like polished steel as he spoke and Frank stiffened and stood still. At first, he grinned, but his smile faded as Delbert's hand stayed steady and the barrel of the Dragoon stared him in the eye. After a tense few seconds Rizzo swallowed tightly and shrugged, "Aw shucks Delbert, why you gotta be so high strung anyhow? This here train ain't yours in the first place, and besides that, as long as we keep feeding her coal, she'll take us anywhere we want to go."

Delbert's hand held the gun in Frank's face for a moment longer, then he slowly put it back in its holster and looked at Frank. "Look, Frank, we don't need to be going out here without a company of soldiers, and you know it. Something is out there, and we is heading straight for it. I signed on to drive a train and help lay track, I didn't sign on to get killed by some spirit, so you just sling that coal and keep yer mouth shut, alright?"

***

Delbert didn't wait for Frank to answer before he returned to the controls. Frank stood there for a moment, fuming and grumbling, but finally reached out with the shovel, opened up the door to the engine furnace, and started throwing shovelfuls of coal into the hungry fire. He stoked it for as long as his arms held up, taking a break every so often to sit back on the jagged lumps of coal to rest, watching the plains slowly roll by and pulling his jacket closer around him as the occasional cold breeze blew in.

***

Timmy was up on top of the coach car, coat pulled up around his ears as he watched the dry, grassy plain ease by beside the train. The cloud of hot gas and cinders that belched from the engine smokestack up ahead would choke and blind him every now and then, but just as quickly move away, depending on the wind direction. He could see the terrain starting to change, and he knew that they must be getting near the gorge as he could see the tall pine trees in the distance up ahead.

Timmy had never been there, but he knew about it from stories. The Cheyenne had been keeping their dead there for as long as anyone could remember. The corpses of the Indians were supposed to be on wooden scaffolds above ground, along with some of their possessions they may need in the afterlife. This was hallowed ground for the Indians; no White man was supposed to disturb it. Even the Indians would not go there unless burying someone, as it was potentially big bad medicine. The spirits of the gorge were said to protect the souls of the dead. There were also rumors of gold in the river that flowed through the gorge, which was one reason the White men had been so hell-bent on laying the railroad through there. It had been hoped that once the railroad was down, prospectors would have easy access to the streams to pan for gold. However, since R&M Rail had laid track through the gorge, enough White men had been killed to ensure it was mostly left well alone now.

Pulling his coat tighter around him against the cold October wind that blew up and out of the gorge and across the plain, Timmy knew he needed to go and remind Ford Smith to check the wheels as Delbert had asked him to. It was getting later in the day, but Timmy was hoping they could make it through the gorge quickly before dark.

Walking across the flat, metal roof of the car, he stopped at the junction between the two cars and climbed down the ladder in the rear of the forward car. Once down, he opened the door to the coach car and went inside.

Shutting the door behind him, he heard someone whisper "Shhhhh!"

As he turned; he saw Ford Smith standing with his finger to his lips. Behind him, Mr. Moore was asleep in his high backed, red-leather chair, snoring loudly, a half-lit cigar still clenched between his teeth. An almost empty bottle of some fancy Sherry sat on the table, attesting that more than just sleep had overtaken the rich Irishman.

Ford motioned for Timmy to follow him as he moved towards the rear of the car and out the door. Once outside, Ford looked at Timmy and grinned slightly. "Looks like the old man had too much to drink; he's passed out cold. I sure hope we can get through the gorge afore he wakes up, or he will be mad as a wet hen. Did you get Frank back on the coal? I bet he was back by the stove drinking and getting warm, wasn't he? I sure hope for your sake that them damn hobos ain't back there!"

As Ford started to move towards the ladder to go up, Timmy moved quickly to the ladder and took hold of it. Turning to Ford, he pointed to the front of the train. "Mr. Jenkins said you need to grease the wheels again, especially the right side. He said it was squeaking something awful, and you got to do it right quick!"

Ford looked at Timmy with his calm but snapping gray eyes wryly for a moment before responding. "Boy, I'm gonna go grease them wheels. Now, it's liable to take me a few hours to get them all done. Hopefully by the time I am done, if there was any hobo on this train, they would have made themselves scarce, you got it?"

Timmy nodded and continued blocking the ladder to the rear of the train. Ford stood looking at Timmy for another moment, then shook his head and turned and went back into the Coach car headed for the front of the train. Breathing a sigh of relief, Timmy climbed up on the roof of the first coach car, then worked his way towards the front of the train. Ford was a Quaker by birth, and a very hard-working man. He was stout, diligent, and had a low tolerance for bandying about with those who didn't pull their weight—which was a slight contradiction to Timmy, considering Ford was always in the coach car with Mr. Moore playing chess, it seemed.

CHAPTER FIVE

The clouds rolled in quickly as the train chugged steadily onwards towards the gorge. Ford had grabbed his tools and grease can, and was up on the front of the engine, working on the rotator mechanism. Greasing a moving train was dangerous work for those who were inexperienced; The huge metal rotators could cut a man in half with no effort, and you could also fall into the wheels and get run over and crushed. Many an engineer or conductor had been killed that way, but Ford was a careful man and had been working steam trains since he was old enough to know what they were, so he had no worries as he moved about the train with ease, loosening up oil caps and injecting the dark brown grease into the ports. The grease was a vital part of the steam train; without it, all the moving parts could rust and seize up at the wrong time, which could disable a train.

***

Timmy stood on the top of the coach car looking at the rapidly approaching gorge as Delbert eased the brass drive lever forwards a notch. The train was picking up some speed, and Timmy loved the rush of air and steam he was caught in. This was as fast a man would ever go, and Timmy felt as though he was king. The plains seemed to be flying by underneath him as the sky moved with him, making the whole of the world seem somehow unreal. Suddenly, he felt a hard bang, heard a screech, and the train suddenly lurched forward, throwing Tommy onto the hard metal roof and knocking the wind out of him. A scream echoed from the front of the train, quickly followed by another—horrible-sounding cries they were—and then silence. Delbert yanked back on the drive lever as hard as he could, putting all his weight on the reverse bar. The train was slowing steadily now, and Delbert began to apply the brakes—Timmy could hear the squeal of the leather and metal pads against the iron engine wheels as they vibrated on the train track. Rizzo had stopped shoveling coal and opened the fire door to quickly let the heat out of the fire box. Tommy stood up shakily, and then moved quickly down the metal ladder to the coal car. As the wheels ground on the rails in their attempt to slow down, Delbert continued straining on the brake lever, veins popping out on his forehead as he attempted to bring the heavy, steaming mass of metal to a halt.

The train finally came to a rest with a loud screech and a huge puff of smoke from the boiler pipe. As it did, all three men lunged around the sides of the engine car and onto the catwalk that ran to the front of the train to see what had happened. As they reached the front edge of the catwalk, Delbert jumped down to the ground, looked at the engine, and suddenly slumped to the ground, his face ashen as he stared at the train. Rizzo had also jumped down and was standing beside Delbert, his face also pale as he stared at the front of the train. As Timmy finally made it down onto the ground, he saw what was to be the first real shock of his life. There was an old railroad tie caught up on the front cattle splitter of the engine, and partially broken chunks of it had wedged in the wheels, but more than that, Ford Smith had been caught up and torn to pieces in the right hand rotator. His head had been crushed to a pulp, and his torso was cut in half. His left leg lay on the ground, along with what looked like his arms. Blood and pieces of what must have been his intestines were everywhere, running down the side of the train. One of his hands had been thrown up on the catwalk, and even in death was clutching, the old metal grease can. Delbert sat frozen on the dry plains grass staring at the body as Rizzo moved over to Ford's arms.

Rizzo gritted his teeth, then reached down and picked up one of the engineer's amputated limbs. "Looks like that damn tie was laying crossways on the tracks when we hit it. Ford musta been throwed into the rotator. Damn Injuns! They done this, trying to sabotage the train coming through. I'll kill every one I get my hands on for this! YOU HEAR ME, INJUNS?!" Rizzo screamed at the gorge up ahead, "I'll KILL EVERY ONE OF YOU SUM'BITCHES!"

Timmy stood still, unsure of how to feel. He had known Ford Smith ever since he had first come to work at the railroad. The man had been in many ways gruff to the young upstart seeking to earn his glory by being on the trains, but he had also taught

Timmy many things about the intricacies of trains and their movement across the ground. The feelings inside Timmy were confusing; he did not know whether to cry or to just continue on with his work. As he continued to struggle with his own internal dilemma, a loud voice rang out from behind them, startling them all.

"What in the name of Sam Hill is goin' on out here? This ain't no damn town meetin'! Whatever it is that's holdin' up the train, git it cleared and let's git goin'!" boomed Robert Moore angrily.

As he stood there, working his cigar from side to side in his mouth as was his habit, Frank Rizzo marched across the ground beside the train with the amputated arm in his hand, coming to stand just below the engine car where Moore was standing. "You're damn right this ain't no town meetin' Mr. High and Mighty! You see what I am holdin' on to? Do you see it? This here's what's left of Ford Smith, the engineer. You know who he was, don't you? He was the man you were playin' chess with this whole godforsaken trip! We hit a railroad tie, and the jolt musta been jest enough to throw him in the rotator. He's all chewed up, jest layin' there!"

***

As Rizzo raged, Delbert had finally stood up, and he moved quickly over to Rizzo and took ahold of his shoulder. Whispering quickly, Delbert tried to calm him down, "Frank, keep yer teeth together or you'll be left sitting out here on the plain. You know he don't care 'bout nobody but hisself, so just hush!"

Rizzo shook off Delbert's restraining hand angrily and raised the dead arm of Ford Smith in his hand like some grotesque protest placard. "So what do you want to do now,

Mr. Moore?" Frank's exaggeration succeeded in getting a quick reaction from the railroad owner.

Robert Moore worked his cigar in his mouth furiously as he glared down at the coal man. "Alright, now you listen up and you listen good. This here train has gotta get moving again, and I mean quick. You clean up whatever it is on the front that's holding us up, and you get it cleared out NOW, you hear me?"

Looking over at Timmy, Moore spoke through gritted teeth, "You boy…Timmy, was that your name? I'm gonna give you five dollars' worth of gold to get that body off my train and buried quick like. He had no family that I know of so there will be no one to mourn him. Now git!" Moore fished a five-dollar gold piece out of the pocket of his waist coat and threw it on the ground by Timmy's feet, then simply turned and moved back towards the coach car, grumbling.

Rizzo started to go up on the train to confront Robert Moore physically, but Delbert restrained him. "Dammit Frank, just settle down. There ain't nothing we kin do for Ford now, so let's git him off the train and buried quick. You go up there and gather up what you can of him, and I will see about getting that tie out from the wheels. Timmy, you go git your shovel out of the rear car and start a grave. That storm is coming, and if we don't get moving quick, we will never get through the gorge before dark hits us. Now MOVE!"

Delbert's uncharacteristic harshness and commanding tone caught both men off guard. After looking at him for a moment as if to make sure he was really the conductor, they both nodded and moved to their tasks. As Delbert pulled and pried to get the broken pieces of timber out from around the wheel, Frank gingerly pulled pieces of broken and bloody body parts from the rotator and the surrounding machinery, piling them on the ground about twenty feet or so from the engine. Delbert noticed he was subconsciously attempting to lay out Ford Smith on the ground as he had been in life— which proved difficult as the body was so mangled. After about thirty minutes, though, he had reassembled a macabre outline of the engineer's body on the grass. Meanwhile, Timmy was already digging the grave, attacking it with is rusty metal shovel almost angrily, making good work of the hole even with the ground being so dry and hard. Delbert himself had removed the jagged railroad tie pieces from around the wheels and the front of the train, having cast their black, creosote coated chunks out the grass beside the engine and was already back over at the controls.

As Frank now, and Timmy took turns digging, Delbert saw something from the corner of his eye. Two men were approaching down the side of the train. He realized who it was in an instant; the two hobos Timmy had been feeding. What were their names, Cotton and Tibbets? He watched as the two shabby men moved over to where Timmy and Frank were digging and stood there for a moment, then Tibbets solemnly took the shovel from Timmy and started digging. After another thirty minutes or so, the grave was dug.

Delbert got the furnace fired up with fresh coal and all the levers primed, then moved down to the grave and stood in silence beside the other four men. Tibbets had laid Ford Smith's body parts down in the grave and was just beginning to cover them with a piece of canvas Timmy had grabbed from one of the club cars. As he patted the dirt he'd just shoveled in down on the top, Cotton picked up some dirt in his hand.

"Ashes to ashes Lord, and dust to dust. This here man's done gone to you now, so be watching out for him, ya hear, Lord? And if any of us come a lookin after him, why, please be lookin' out for us too. Amen." With that, Cotton let the dirt fall from between his wrinkled fingers down on the grave slowly. All five stood there with bowed heads for a minute, then slowly turned and moved back to the train.

Their grief over what had happened remained unspoken; Ford's death had come so quickly that all the men appeared to be in a state of shock. Well, except for one. Delbert got the sense that Frank Rizzo was just angry. He was angry at the Indians who he thought had caused the death, and he was angry at the railroad owner, Robert Moore, for his indifference. In his mind burned nothing but revenge on anyone that he could lay blame to, and this Delbert was sure of.

Delbert watched Rizzo move back to the coal car silently. He knew there was unrest there now and it worried him. He also watched Timmy as he followed the hobos back to the rear car, the three men moving slowly down the tracks. Shaking his head, he thought about how Timmy somehow reminded him of himself at that age; unsure of life and confused about who he was but hugely caring. Delbert smiled slightly; Timmy would learn some good lessons from the hobos at least.

As Delbert saw the three men climb aboard the caboose, he climbed up the heavy iron ladder into the engine car. Taking his place on the worn wooden seat just behind the controls, he reached forward and released the red wheel brake control lever, and then slowly eased back on the long brass drive bar. The train belched its smoky response, sending a huge plume of smoke and cinder up into the sky, then another, and another. The train roughly eased forward with the loud chugging sound Delbert had grown to love more than life itself over the years.

The train was his wife. Miss Emily—as he called her—was a better partner than any he had ever had, being more dependable than any woman he knew except for his now dead squaw wife. He had taken care of this train and she had taken care of him.

Looking out at the horizon, Delbert could see the huge storm clouds drawing near. It was going to be a bad one he thought and that was something they did not need now. He took a quick glance at his stopwatch, and then he leaned out and looked ahead to the gorge with a painfully slow sigh. They were not going to make it. They had lost too much time now. Darkness and the storm were going to catch them in the Dead Gorge.

CHAPTER SIX

The train was moving at a steady slow pace now and the click of the wheels as they hit each rail spike was a rhythm that seldom changed. Back in the caboose, all three men sat in the cozy warmth by the potbellied stove as the lull of the train made all three somewhat drowsy. But none could sleep after what had happened.

"That there is bad medicine Timmy, you mark my words. The engineer dyin' like that don't bode well for the rest of us." Cotton spoke in a hushed tone, and looked over at Tibbets, who nodded his agreement with a scared cast to his eyes. The Black mute made some signs with his hands for a few minutes as Cotton studied him intently.

Timmy watched in silence at first, then finally spoke up, "Cotton, what is he a sayin'?"

Cotton turned his head and looked at Timmy for a moment, then turned back to the stove and started to get a pipe ready. "Timmy, that ol' Tibbets knows quite a bit about death and other things. The way he figures it, this train is marked. This whole *railroad* is marked. Cuttin' across the Injuns territory was bad enough, but when Mr. Moore went and disturbed all them graves out yonder in that gorge, well…Something mighty bad is going to happen if we keep going. Tibbets here figures we oughta get offen this here train and walk back to the post."

Timmy shook his head from side to side fervently, "There ain't no way we could make it back to the post on foot from way out here, Cotton! It's too far, not to mention any Indians that spot us won't take too kindly to us being out here in the first place. This is their land. They might not ask no questions; just kill us. We gotta stay on the train. I know Mr. Jenkins will get us through the gorge and to the rail head. He was hired for just that and he knows this train and what he's doing. We got to give him the chance!"

Cotton drew slowly on his pipe as he watched the wooden match he had lit it with between his fingers burn down. As the flame slowly died out, he considered how like flames people were. They all started out with a bright spark, burning intensely for their brief moment of life, then as they reached the end, all things grew cold and died.

He dropped the match to the floor and looked at Timmy. "Well Timmy, I reckon this here train is movin' too fast for me and ol' Tibbets to jump off of anyhow, but you let this train stop and me and him are gettin' out of here, you understand? If you don't come with us, it has been nice knowin' you boy." He reached over and gripped Timmy on the shoulder with a strong hand, looking intently into the young boy's eyes. Smiling,

Cotton leaned back and started humming a little tune to himself. Tibbets had closed his eyes and leaned back on the wall with his booted feet to the stove for warmth.

Timmy got up and pulled his coat around himself as he started to go back up to the front of the train. "Cotton, I reckon if the train stops again, I might be obliged to go with you'uns. Maybe I ain't cut out for train riding though. Maybe I oughta go be a cowboy or something," Timmy said with a weak grin.

Cotton simply looked at the boy and winked. With that, Timmy went through the door of the caboose and headed back up the ladder to the top of the train.

***

Walking slowly towards the front of the moving behemoth, Timmy looked at the surrounding countryside, casting his eyes either side of the train nervously. The pale, golden prairie grass stretched as far as the eye could see; all the way to the huge, dark thunderclouds that were so close now he could see lightning flashing in them. Looking ahead, the mountains around the gorge were not far away at all now. The sun was going down rapidly, and Timmy knew that they would be pressed to make it through the long gorge before dark set in entirely. As he dropped down onto the freight car he checked the chains in the flatbeds again, then as he was moving among the stacked iron rails and timber, he noticed something lying partially under one of the railroad ties. He leaned down between one of the huge bundles, bent close and had to strain to reach it. His fingers touched it once, and then he was able to grasp it. Pulling it out, he stood there for a moment examining it. Dangling from his fingers by an old leather strap was a small doll made out of bits of straw and leather. It had some brightly colored bits of stone for eyes, and the head was made out of doeskin. What appeared to be dried plant juice stained it a dark color almost all over. It appeared to be attached to a necklace of some sort and was obviously of Indian make.

How did it get here?

Timmy's brows furrowed in thought over the trinket laying in a place it should not have been, but at this point, trying to figure out where it came from would have to wait. Timmy was about to throw it off the train when for some reason, he decided to put the leather string around his neck and tuck the doll into the front of his coveralls.

He continued to move through the flatbeds as quick as he could, checking the chains and ropes for any looseness and looking for any other stray items that might have found their way onto the train. Reaching the rear of the second coach car, he climbed the metal ladder and moved onto the shaking metal roof. The roof was preferable to passing through the carriages, as he did not want to come into contact with Mr. Moore again if he could help it. Walking across the roofs of the cars, he noticed that they had reached the scattered pine and locust trees on the outer edge of the gorge, and could feel the cold breath of the storm brewing. He would have to get under cover soon, as the rain could start at any moment.

He moved quickly along the roofs then jumped down into the coal car and moved through the black rocks to reach the rear of the engine car. Rizzo was resting on his shovel, breathing heavily and Mr. Jenkins was holding onto the drive bar, looking out the window ahead.

As he moved near the men, Timmy could feel Rizzo glaring at him. "Did you tell them hobos to get off the train the next time we stop, Timmy? They got no business aboard!" Rizzo snapped angrily.

Timmy knew Frank was still fuming over Ford's death and Mr. Moore's indifference, and he did not want to aggravate him any further. "Yessir, I done told them that once we stop, they have to get off."

Rizzo snorted and looked away as if he didn't believe what Timmy had said.

By this time, Delbert had turned, and was in the process of saying something to Frank when a loud crash resounded. The train suddenly jerked sideways and slowed rapidly, throwing all the men forward onto their hands and knees.

Cursing and spitting out dust and blood where his mouth had hit the metal floor, Rizzo stood up and yelled, "Goddamn A'mighty, Jenkins, what happened now?"

Also spitting dust and rubbing his sleeve across his now-flushed face, Delbert Jenkins stood up and looked around. The train was making a loud screeching noise from the front wheels and the whole engine was shuddering. "Timmy, you go up the catwalk. Be careful, but take a looksee. I'm gonna get us stopped." As he spoke, Delbert reached up and pulled the brake bar back easily, and then closed the drive bar back into neutral. The train chugged and puffed a few times, slowly coming to a rolling stop after about a hundred feet with a loud hiss of steam, a groan from the brakes, and a final belch of smoke.

***

As Timmy worked his way around the side of the engine, Rizzo moved over to the furnace door and opened it to check on the fire pit, then shut the door slightly. The cold in the air was growing as the storm got closer, and the heat from the coal fire was welcome. Delbert had set the brake and had returned all the controls to neutral. As he checked the gauges, everything seemed to be in working order. He glanced at the thermometer on the side of the control panel. The temperature had dropped to almost freezing in just an hour; he had checked it before, and it was on 58 degrees. Frowning at the sudden drop, he pulled his coat tighter around him and stamped his feet a little. Looking over at Frank who was shoveling the coal back away from the furnace following the small avalanche caused by the sudden stop, he cleared his throat and spoke quietly. "Dangit Frank, it done got cold all of a sudden, don't you think? Heck, it's dang near freezing now. What do you make of that?"

Frank kept shoveling coal, but as he did, he replied gruffly, "Don't make no knowhow to me Delbert, all I know is we done stopped again, and if you didn't take notice, we are in the Dead Gorge, and that there is not where we need to be. You know who is gonna come bustin' through up here and blame us for another delay. And shore as the day I'm gonna get fired, cause I'm gonna punch Ol' Money Bags in the nose! I've had about enough of his lip on this trip!" As he finished, Rizzo threw his shovel on the floor of the coal car and turned towards the gang ladder going down the side of it.

"Where are you going, Frank?" Delbert asked nervously.

"I'm going to go up and see if I can see what is going on with Timmy. We gots to get this train moving again, and fast!"

***

Rizzo moved over to the ladder and climbed down to the ground. He turned and looked towards the rear of the train for a moment. Seeing nothing out of the ordinary, he turned and started walking towards the front of the engine. Something about the trees on either side of the train made him nervous. He thought about going and getting the rifle that was in the coach car, but decided he had better not risk running into Moore.

As he reached the front of the train, he saw Timmy standing there staring at the tracks with his hands in his pockets. "Goddamn Timmy, if you ain't a kick in the nuts! Why are you just standing there? Just get to…" Rizzo trailed off as he reached the front of the engine and saw what Timmy was looking at. The iron rail on one side of the tracks had been pulled loose and was bent outward, and the damage went all the way back to where they had first heard the bang. Timmy turned to Rizzo and spoke nervously, "Frank, you see that? Something done pulled the track up on this side; even the spikes are bent out! Did we do that?"

Frank shook his head from side to side, "No boy, we didn't do that. If we would have hit a shifted track, we would have run off the rail and probably turned over. This here track has been bent on purpose, it looks like, but how could them Injuns have bent this track and then laid it back down again? Don't make no sense!"

After looking around and up for a while, Frank turned to Timmy with a cold stare. "Timmy, there ain't nothing we can do but roll the train back and then swap out that rail. It's gonna take every one of us to git a new rail offen the flatbed and git this one changed out. We got the tools to do it, but it's getting dark quick with that storm coming. You light out quick, git them hobos and tell them they gonna have to work for their trip this time. Tell Mr. Moore he is going to have to help to if he wants his train moved. Now go!"

***

Frank's harsh words startled Timmy into action. Timmy jumped across the tracks and headed down the other side of the train towards the rear. As he passed the engineer's roost, Delbert saw him run by and yelled down to him, "Timmy, what on Earth is going on? Where are you running to?"

"The track is bent out, Mr. Jenkins, Rizzo says we gots to replace it. I am going to go get Mr. Moore and Cotton and Tibbets to help. Frank says it's gonna take all of us to get the rail swapped out!" Timmy yelled out as he ran by.

As Timmy sped towards the rear of the train, he could see it growing steadily darker around them as the storm clouds moved in. There was no rain yet, but the cold was enough that Timmy thought they should see snow at any moment. He ran straight back to the caboose, went up the now freezing metal ladder, and jerked the door open quickly. Going inside, he found Cotton and Tibbets both looking fearfully out the window on the other side.

"Cotton, what in the blazes are you two…?" Timmy trailed off as Cotton held up his shaking, wrinkled old hand. Cotton turned, looking whiter that Timmy had ever seen the dirty old hobo look before. Cotton held a finger to his lips to quiet him, then motioned him over to the window. As Timmy walked over, he could see sweat running down the side of Tibbets' face, which made no sense. It was cold in the caboose even with the small fire going.

When he reached the window, Cotton pointed and whispered in Timmy's ear, "Boy, there is something out there in them trees, and it ain't Injuns. Tibbets saw it a few minutes ago, and all he keeps saying is 'demon'. I can't make no sense of it."

As Timmy turned towards the mute, Tibbets looked at him, and Timmy could see raw fear in his eyes. Sweat was pouring off the Black man's forehead and running down his cheeks almost like tears. With a shaking finger, Tibbets pointed out towards the forest and grimaced. Timmy put his hand on Tibbets's shoulder and squeezed quickly in an attempt to calm him...and himself.

Looking out the window, Timmy saw nothing but the dark clouds covering everything. It had grown so gloomy outside that the trees were merging into the clouds as if being sucked into some kind of eerie vortex. He turned to Cotton and whispered, "Cotton, we gots to get one of them rails replaced on the tracks. Something has done bent one so far out that we can't go on. Mr. Rizzo says it's gonna take all of us to do it. I gots to go get Mr. Moore too!"

Cotton shook his head from side to side. "Boy, there ain't no way we gonna git one of them rails down offrn that flatbed, never mind drug up to the front of the train!"

"Frank says we all is going to do it, Cotton. He says it's time you'uns paid for your trip and he means it. Please Cotton, we gotta do this. Now you and Tibbets come on down the right side of the train. I didn't see nothing in them woods, and Hell, it was probably a bear or wolf or something anyhow."

As he finished speaking, Tibbets turned and grabbed him by the hand. Raising Timmy's hand in front of Timmy's face, Tibbets folded down all but two of Timmy's fingers, then made a walking motion with his own fingers in the air in front of their faces. There was nothing but utter terror in the Black man's eyes. Timmy coughed for a second then spoke quietly "You mean something out there was walking on two legs, Tibbets?"

Tibbets nodded quickly.

"Well shoot, could have been an Indian at that. Don't matter none, we gots to get out of here quick. It's getting dark and we're in the gorge. We gots no choice! Ya'll gots to come on." Timmy turned and went out the caboose door, pausing long enough to turn and look at the two hobos. Making eye contact with them both, Timmy nodded then turned and moved down the ladder to the ground.

CHAPTER SEVEN

Grumbling to himself, Cotton turned and grabbed his raggedy jacket from off the cracker box beside the stove and started putting it on. Tibbets grabbed Cotton's arm, shaking his head from side to side wildly. Cotton looked at him solemnly. "Now dangit Tibbets, we ain't got no choice. This here train ain't gonna move and whether we help fix it or we clear outta here, we got to move. Now you can stay here like some old woman or you can be a man and come on!" With that, Cotton put on his coat and went out the door behind Timmy.

Tibbets reached and picked up his old, stained brown coat off the floor and put it on slowly. Reaching into the pocket, he pulled out a small, worn, black leather Bible. Raising it up to his lips, he kissed the cover once and then put it back in his jacket. He moved through the door and then shut it behind him.

***

As the three men moved along the side of the train towards the coach cars, the cold wind whipping off the plains behind them was like the icy fingers of death come to claim them. As they passed the flatbeds, Timmy looked up at the iron track stacked neatly on the freight car racking. For some reason, as he passed, he thought that one of the chains on this side seemed loose but paid no more thought to it as they reached the first coach car.

As dark as it now was outside, Timmy expected to see the oil lamps lit inside the cars, but both cars were completely dark. As he reached up to grip the ladder to the rear coach car, Cotton stayed his hand for a moment.

"Timmy, you best be letting me go in first and make sure everything is OK."

Timmy smiled. "Cotton, you old fool, don't you think you traipsing in there on Mr. Moore in the dark is liable to get you shot? I'll be fine; anyhow, I got my knife." Timmy pulled the long, store bought knife out of its sheath on his waist and held it up, as if the bone handled knife would somehow ward off anything. Cotton shook his head, but let Timmy move up the ladder first. Once on the platform, Timmy opened the door and went inside.

CHAPTER EIGHT

Frank cursed as he shoveled rocks from around the railroad ties. He was trying to get the track cleared out enough so that he could get to the spikes and the bent rail. Luckily, they would not have to move the train back any further; it had come to rest on the other side of the split. They should be able to replace this section and then the weight of the train should help ease them on over without further problems.

Delbert had walked out on the railing to the front of the engine and was watching Rizzo shovel. As he stood there, something moving caught the corner of his eye. He couldn't see what it was, but it had been in the trees just in back of Rizzo. Rather than stop Frank from doing his work, Delbert decided to go check it out for himself. Drawing his pistol, he made sure it was cocked and ready, and then he moved down the ladder to the ground.

Looking out at the trees for a moment to make sure there was nothing visible there, he moved slowly towards the forest. He covered the hundred or so feet between where he had been standing and the edge of the trees quickly, then, gritting his teeth against the now freezing air, he plunged into the woods.

***

Rizzo was so busy shoveling and trying to pull the spikes up with his pry bar that he never saw Delbert move out into the woods. It was starting to get darker now, so he stopped for a quick breather and decided to get an oil lamp going on the front of the train for light. He climbed up the cattle grate to the huge globe on the left side of the train, raised the sooty yellowed glass, and reached in with a match to light the oil wick. Slowly, the flame licked hungrily at the cotton wick, then finally took hold and started to flare up. Rizzo lowered the globe and turned the wick up about a half inch so it would give out plenty of light. Climbing back down to the ground, he returned to his task of clearing the rocks away from the rail.

He worked for about thirty minutes or so, as the light from the lamp up on the front of the train cast an eerie yellow ring around him. By now, he had cleared most of the track, and was in the process of pulling out the spikes. One was particularly stubborn, so he got down on all fours to try and work it loose. As he concentrated on the spike, he noticed he was having a hard time seeing it. There should have been ample light coming from the huge oil lamp, but for some reason, it had grown dark.

As he turned, his mind never had time to grasp the fact that something huge was standing there blocking the light. It was a creature, massive, and it stood on two legs but in a peculiar crouching way. As Frank's eyes met those of this beast, the shock of what it was never registered. As his mouth moved in an attempt to scream, the massive hairy arm of the creature swung in a wide arc and impacted the side of Frank's head. His skull was instantly crushed, and then ripped from his shoulders. Blood sprayed everywhere as his body crumpled to the tracks, twitching violently for a few seconds, his legs kicking at different angles, and then slowly they slowly stilled. The eyes of the creature burned with a hideous, bestial red fire, but surrounding them, was the twisted, broken face of an Indian, distorted with rage and hatred. The bones of its skull were massive, yet no symmetry was found anywhere on its face. Its mouth opened to reveal a row of yellow, jagged teeth, manlike and yet also like those of some great bear. It reached down, grabbed the body of Frank Rizzo in its huge, clawed hands and picked it up as though it were straw. It threw the body over its shoulders and then leapt for the forest on the other side of the tracks with blinding speed, vanishing among the gloom and trees.

***

Timmy and Cotton edged along inside the coach car, barely able to see in the darkened gloom. They passed a few rows of seats, seeing nothing out of the ordinary, so Timmy decided to light one of the oil lamps on the wall to make things easier to see. He moved over to it and lifted the small, glass globe from on top of the lamp. Striking a match, he held it to the wick, which caught instantly. Lowering the globe, Timmy turned up the wick slightly as the dull light spread to the inside of the car.

"Lord Almighty," Timmy heard Cotton mumble quietly.

As Timmy turned back towards the front of the car, he saw Cotton frozen as if in shock in the middle of the aisle. Timmy looked past Cotton and saw what had caused the hobo to pause so quickly. There, on top of the gaming table, was the head of Mr. Moore, a railroad spike driven through it. Blood was everywhere, and the look on Moore's face was enough to make Timmy's blood run cold. His eyes held a look of abject horror, as if in his final moments he had recognized his killer, and been frightened to death in the instant his head was ripped off.

Cotton's hands shook as he reached over and picked up the rifle leaning up against the wall. "Ain't no shots been fired outta here, Timmy." Cotton said as he inspected the chamber of the 30/30 carbine. "Still loaded too. Whatever did this didn't make no sound; and Moore never had time to scream, or if he did, no one heard it!" hissed Cotton in a strained voice.

Timmy turned around to see Tibbets standing there shaking so hard it was as if he was having convulsions. He held onto a small black Bible so hard that his hands were beginning to turn white. Timmy gritted his teeth against the panic that was rising within him and spoke quietly, "Tibbets, calm down man! Whatever did this is probably long gone. Maybe you oughta go back to the caboose and wait for us there. We are going to go forward to the front of the train and get Mr. Jenkins and Mr. Rizzo."

As Timmy finished, Tibbets shook his head slightly in agreement and turned back to the door of the coach car. Passing through it quickly, he was gone. Timmy turned back to Cotton, as the old hobo just stared at the head of the railroad owner in shock. Timmy moved woodenly—still not understanding what was going on—towards the front of the car. Cotton followed right behind him, the rifle now clutched in his shaking hands.

***

Delbert Jenkins was a very simple and patient man, but he was also strong, with a clear sense of duty. They had to get the train back on the rail and get moving. Mr. Moore had entrusted this job to him, and he was going to finish it. He knew Frank would take care of the rail with the help of the other four men; he just had to make sure the perimeter of the train was safe from Injuns. He didn't feel like getting an arrow in the gut while he was working on the tracks. If there were any Injuns about, he would find them.

Making sure his Dragoon pistol was still cocked and ready, Delbert moved through the woods along the edge of the tracks, parallel to the train. As he moved through the tangled brush, deadfall and trees, he realized that it was almost completely dark now. He could barely make out the light coming from the front of the train—but the light meant that Frank must have lit the storm lamp on the front of the engine. He was about even with the caboose now and had not seen or heard anything yet. He was in the process of turning when a limb snapped behind him. Delbert froze; for he knew that sound. Something heavy had stepped on a twig, and it had broken under its weight.

Sweat broke out on his forehead as he stood still in the darkness, his ears straining for any other movement in the underbrush. He also noticed a foul smell beginning to creep through the wood. Upon that reek hitting his nose, he breathed an angry sigh of relief for a moment. "Just a dang polecat! I'm out here in the dang cold and dark getting spooked by a skunk. Dangit, Timmy, you and them daggum stories done got me all flusterated. I've a good mind to put that boy to shoveling coal for the rest of the trip." Delbert huffed to himself.

He moved further away from the smell and where he had heard the twig snap, feeling his way along through the trees and fallen logs and moving slowly as to not make too much noise. Suddenly he felt cold—colder that he had ever felt before, and with that cold came an instant, instinctive fear. The hair stood up on the back of his neck involuntarily and he could feel his legs shaking uncontrollably. As he took a step, he heard something fall behind him, almost as if his step had been echoed. He took another step and heard the same thing. Something heavy was moving with each step he took. Sweat was pouring off his forehead now, even though the cold was making his teeth chatter. He could hear whatever it was moving behind him in the dark, coming through the trees with deliberate, menacing steps. Delbert decided discretion was the better part of valor, and he thought to move toward the train as quickly as possible. As he did, he heard the most horrible low growl not twenty feet behind him, and it made his blood freeze in his veins. As he started to run, he could hear limbs breaking and twigs snapping now as whatever animal it was, moved with no hesitation towards him. Delbert was no longer calm and collected, he openly sobbed as he tried to get away from the horrible, unseen force behind him in the dark of the trees. Just as he reached the edge of the tree line and the open plain between him and the train, he was suddenly jerked off his feet as a huge, clawed hand went completely through his back and exited his chest, then lifted him four feet in the air. Delbert's mouth struggled in an attempt to scream. He could see the light from the oil lamp in the coach car. Surely someone had to see him and would come to his aid? Nothing escaped his lips though, except a crimson froth as the life blood from his fluttering heart pumped freely into his throat. As he struggled weakly, the creature that had impaled him turned Delbert Jenkins around until he looked full into its eyes. Delbert's own eyes widened in shock—in his final moment, he realized that the red war paint on the distorted cheek of this thing meant it was no animal…

***

Timmy and Cotton had made it through the final coach car and had moved onto the back of the coal car. Climbing up the metal ladder on the back of the coal bin, they eased over onto the mound of dusty rocks and slid towards the bottom. Cotton gripped the rifle in his hand tightly, looking nervously out at the edge of the forest. As they reached the bottom of the mound, Cotton cleared his throat and Timmy turned around.

"Timmy, you go on up and find the conductor and Rizzo and tell em what has happened. You tell them to git up here lickety split and git armed. I don't think we is gonna be able to fix this here train!" Cotton's eyes were wild with fear and uncontrolled panic, but he gritted his teeth as he leaned the rifle barrel over the top of the coal car rail towards the forest. "I'm gonna stand here and keep a lookout until you get back. Looks like somebody fired that oil lamp up front, so that's where there probably are. Keep a sharp eye out, boy!"

Timmy nodded and turned toward the ladder. Throwing his leg over the side, he went down two rungs, then stopped and looked at Cotton. The old hobo looked at the woods and gripped the rifle so tightly that his knuckles turned white with the strain. He looked at Timmy, managed a slight smile and a wink, then moved his eyes back to the forest.

Timmy moved down the rough metal rungs of the ladder slowly. As he reached the ground, he turned slightly to look back down the train towards the caboose. He thought for a moment that he saw a dark shape near the rear of the train, but it was so hazy that he could have been mistaken. He turned and started walking towards the light at the front of the engine. Walking along the edge of the tracks was hard at times, due to the uneven nature of the gravel beside the tracks. He finally reached the edge of the light shadow being cast on the ground, but no one was there. He walked across to the other side of the track and looked quickly from side to side.

"Frank? Mr. Jenkins? Are you out there?" Timmy called nervously but quietly into the dark. Hearing nothing, Timmy's stomach started to churn wildly, and he could feel himself sweating profusely under his clothes, even though the wind was freezing now. As he turned to go back around the front of the engine, he spotted something odd; Rizzo's shovel and pry bar were laying crossways on the track as if he had dropped them.

Timmy moved then bent over to pick them up…and it's then he saw the blood. There was blood everywhere; on the rocks, the rails, and all over the shovel. Timmy froze, not knowing what to do, his feet planted in the gravel. He managed to slowly stand up after a few minutes, but stood stiff with fear. His teeth were chattering worse now, but not with the cold. Absolute fear had entered him, and it was gripping tight on his heart; which he could feel beating so hard he thought it would burst. He gritted his teeth and turned slowly towards the rear of the train. He started shuffling his feet in an attempt to make his way back to Cotton when suddenly he heard a loud gunshot, then another. Cotton was shooting at something!

Timmy strained his eyes in the dark to see where Cotton was, and then, out of the dim shadows, a nightmarishly huge creature came sprinting across the ground, racing towards the train. Tommy was suddenly immobile with terror, and he felt the warm release of his urine run down his legs as his bladder involuntarily gave up. From where he stood, trembling, Timmy watched as the beast leapt across the ground with huge bounds. It ran on two feet like a man, but it was not a man. Long, stringy black hair with a single braid flowed from a head that was massive and human like, and it was covered slightly in places with dark brown hair. It looked to be at least 8 feet tall with heavily muscled arms ending in clawed, manlike hands. Cotton was yelling and firing wildly now. Timmy thought he heard one or two slugs hit the creature, but it made no apparent difference. Timmy watched in horror as the creature closed the distance between itself and the train and leapt in the air, coming down on Cotton, crushing the hobo to the floor of the coal car. Timmy heard the most horrible growls and roars, followed by one more gunshot as Cotton screamed so terribly that Timmy started to cry uncontrollably. Then…silence.

As he stood there unmoving with tears flowing down his cheeks for what seemed like hours, Timmy's thoughts were in chaos. He knew he had to get out of there, but his legs wouldn't move an inch. Whatever that thing was, it had apparently killed everyone. This was the beast that Cotton had spoken of…and Cotton had paid the price for that blasphemy, it seemed, as had Rizzo and Mr. Jenkins and Mr. Moore. Timmy struggled with his own mental collapse for a minute longer, but as his hands reached up to his chest to subconsciously pull his coat tighter against the cold, they touched the necklace he had found, and suddenly his mind cleared. He had to get to the rear of the train and lock himself in the caboose. Mr. Moore had bragged about how it had been reinforced to prevent robberies, the doors and walls being extra thick as well as there being bars on the windows.

    Timmy wheeled around in a flash and darted across the tracks to the other side of the train. He was going to sprint down the opposite side from where that thing had killed Cotton; and hopefully it would still be occupied so he could slip past. As he reached the grass on the other side of the train, Timmy's legs pumped furiously. He didn't stop as he passed by the coal car. Whatever was transpiring in there; he didn't want to know. The tears on his cheeks dried in the crisp air that was blowing past him now, and the cold was forgotten. He had almost reached the second flatbed when he saw one of the rails sticking out off the side of the car. Too late to stop, Timmy ran full tilt into the end of the iron railing. It caught him in a glancing blow on the side of the head, and pain exploded in a bright light that immediately turned into black unconsciousness.

CHAPTER NINE

Tibbets ran along the tracks as fast as his legs would carry him. He would stumble and fall every few feet, tripping over the uneven square railroad ties. He clutched his Bible as he ran like a shield, hoping to ward off the evil behind him and mumbled as tears streamed freely down his face. He had gone about half a mile in the darkness away from the train when he heard gunshots behind him. Whatever was going on back there now, fear had taken hold of him, and he was not stopping. His sole thought was on getting as far away from that train and the gorge as possible. Injuns be damned, he wasn't going to get eat up by some monster. His feet were bleeding now, as his boots had come off in his flight over the tracks, but he paid no notice to the pain.

Whimpering with the sheer and utter terror, he didn't see the huge black shape rise up out of the grass in front of him until he was almost on it…then it was too late. With a strangled moan, Tibbets tried to stop, but the beast merely held out a huge, clawed hand and drove it through Tibbets' eye sockets. The man twitched violently as the terrible demon lifted him completely off the tracks and shook him like a dog would a rat. Tibbets's spasms finally subsided, and he hung there, impaled on the hand of this massive evil thing, blood dripping down his chest and onto the Bible still clutched in his now lifeless hand.

The beast tilted its bestial yet somehow manlike head back, and was about to howl into the night when it threw its head down suddenly, its baleful red eyes lighting up. It sensed something else now, something close by. Dropping the dead man with a shake of its wrist, it bounded down the tracks towards the train, eyes flashing again but with a different purpose now.

FINAL CHAPTER

Timmy was aware only of a shaking sensation. In his mind, he knew that he was dead, so whatever was shaking him must be the creature eating him. He felt a huge pain in his head that would not stop pounding, but there was something else…he heard a voice calling to him. Was it Cotton? Mr. Jenkins? Timmy's mind struggled to come out of the fog of his death, but after a few seconds more, the voice became plainer and more understandable.

"Timmy, you must wake now! Get up, we must go!" The voice was familiar, but it couldn't be…?

Timmy struggled to open his heavy, bruised eyes. As each lid opened, he could only see a foggy haze at first, but then there was something else. A faintly familiar face loomed above him. Timmy tried to raise himself to a sitting position but fell back again. Strong hands lifted him up, and he could feel a damp cloth being wiped across his eyes. As he opened them again, the scene became clearer, and he struggled for a moment in fear. There were six Cheyenne braves standing around him as a seventh wiped his forehead.

He fought with his urge to get up and run as the words of the one in front of him finally registered in his already overstressed mind. "Timmy, it is I, Two Fox. We are not here to harm you, but you must get up, now! Yashewe comes!"

Timmy was in shock. His friend from so long ago was in front of him, talking to him as if they were still friends and he was alive. His mind was almost on the verge of total collapse. He numbly struggled to gain his feet as Two Fox helped him up. The other Cheyenne looked around nervously at the surrounding plains, all with their rifles and bows at the ready for some reason. As Timmy reached his feet and stood there shakily, Two Fox was already motioning for his horse to be brought over. Once the white painted horse was close, he helped Timmy put his hands on it to steady himself. As he did, the other horses snorted and squealed, and the men started yelling and whooping. Timmy's eyes flew open as a huge creature materialized out of the plains behind them. It rose to full height and towered over the men even on horseback as its hairy, muscled arms flexed slowly. Two Fox was chanting and holding out a small totem with his arms up towards the creature. Timmy then realized that Two Fox was holding the same type of figure that Timmy himself had on the necklace around his neck. The beast was growling and making horrible noises, and drool was dripping down its chest. Its mouth was open, teeth bared at the Cheyenne braves.

Two Fox kept up the chanting as one of the other braves jumped back down to help Timmy get up onto the horse. As Timmy struggled to keep his seat, Two Fox jumped up behind him, still chanting. The other braves all moved their horses slowly away towards the forest; never taking their eyes off the thing they called Yashewe. Timmy sat there, dumbfounded and in shock as Two Fox chanted the beast's name and then tossed the figure in his hand over to it. Yashewe caught the small totem doll in its huge, clawed hand. It looked intently at Two Fox for a moment, then slowly turned and headed back into the plains. Two Fox turned his pony towards the forest and the other retreating braves and dug his heels in. The horse trotted forward at an even pace as Timmy bounced in front trying desperately to hold on, his head pounding. The whole thing seemed like a dream somehow.

"Two Fox…how…who…what is going on?" Timmy slurred.

Two Fox pulled Timmy closer to him and made sure he was secure on the front of the horse as they rode away from the train. "You have come through much, Timmy, my brother, but you are alive. We were returning from a hunting party when we heard the gunshots near the gorge. We found the train, and you. This was brought on by the white man's greed, and all shall pay for it. Yashewe protects these lands, and we fear him. He was a warrior long ago that gave up his spirit to protect those who had died and our sacred lands. He didn't appear until the White man came and tore up the sacred burial grounds with their trains. You are safe now, Timmy. You will live with us and learn the ways of the Cheyenne. Do not go back to the White man or Yashewe will hunt you down. You have the sacred Cochina, and it is you who must tell this tale to the sons and their sons. Do you understand, Timmy?"

As Two Fox finished speaking, they heard a loud, guttural cry from out on the plains behind them; a cry that was half-human, half-beast and it drove their blood cold. The horse sped up its pace as Two Fox held the leather reins in check.

Timmy shuddered, both from the cold and the fear that was still in his heart. "Two Fox, I do not know what has happened, but I will go with you and do as you ask. You saved me from the beast when you could have passed me by. I am forever in your debt" Tears streamed down his cheeks as he slumped forward on the horse and held on as they moved across the grass.

Two Fox gripped his blood brother Timmy on the shoulder and smiled slightly as they rode into the night behind the other Cheyenne braves…

***

Endnote: New York, November 1st, 1867.

"Mr. Munroe, a telegram for you, sir," the young boy in the smart red jacket said in a nervous voice, as he handed over an envelope in his hand to the large, smiling Scotsman who was dressed in a dark green kilt and dress jacket. He was sitting at green felt card table surrounded by two beautiful women in brightly colored gowns and two men in black suits.

"Thank you, lad. Here is a dollar for you, now be on your way," the Scotsman boomed as he handed the boy a silver coin. Still smiling, he turned to his companions, "It appears to be a telegram from that most annoying bastard Robert Moore; I presume to tell me he has reached the checkpoint and is needing some more of my money. That greedy Irish son of a cur refuses to spend his own money on the train, saying it needs to go to the Pope or something, and that my money is what will drive the train across America. What a load of rubbish! Why, if I was in my right mind, I would…"

Munroe trailed off as his eyes scanned the telegram intently, the smile dropping slowly from his face. After a few seconds, he dropped the telegram onto the table and got up, a blank stare on his face. He moved over to the bar and quietly ordered a large scotch whiskey, downing the contents of the glass in an instant.

***

As he stood staring at the mirror behind the bar with the empty glass clutched in his hand, the woman in the bright blue dress at the table laughed nervously, "What in the world caused that, do you think? Beverly, be a dear and read the telegram. I don't think Jacob would mind."

The petit blonde woman in the yellow dress nodded nervously and reached over and picked up the telegram as the two men in black suits leaned forward to listen. Beverly's eyes widened as she started to read the telegram, her voice faltering:

"To Jacob Munroe, owner R&M Railroad, Stop. Robert Moore murdered, Stop. All employees bound for outland gorge depot presumed dead or missing, Stop. Horrible mutilations left, no burial remains, Stop. Train demolished in crash over gorge tracks, nothing salvageable, Stop. Suspect Southern bandits or highwaymen behind atrocities as Black hobo found crucified on two railroad timbers not far from wreck, Stop. Send word with new instructions on moving railroad tracks forward, Stop. Signed. Captain James Aubry, Commanding, Frontier Post 314, Stop..."

About the Author

S.D. McGuire is a Scottish-born Celt with Viking roots who began writing horror at the age of twelve. Among his talents, he has been a dish washer, chef, garage mechanic, motorcycle racer as well as having served 10 years in the military. S.D. McGuire fought in the Middle East and Bosnia and traveled extensively around the world. From his voyages, he has amassed an imagination for the macabre that spans centuries. He continues to write his own blend of horror and sci-fi, and currently resides on the east coast of the USA.

About the Illustrator

Erick "Dub" Weir is a talented tattoo artist who hails from Phoenix, AZ. He enjoys sketching dark fantasy art in his spare time. Erick was most recently a creature concept artist for the 2019 film "The Head Hunter".

To learn more about Erick, find him on Instagram @dubweir.

Lightning Source UK Ltd.
Milton Keynes UK
UKHW020740100320
360091UK00011B/313